No Worries
[a book of ocean poems]

written • Amanda Gehrke AND Allison Sojka • pictures

LUMINOSITY PRESS

To our three favorite fishes at home:

Chloe, Ella & Avry

And our
wonderful husbands:

Jeff & Steven

No Worries Whale: a book of ocean poems
Copyright © 2013 by Luminosity Press
Text copyright © 2013 by Amanda Gehrke
Illustrations copyright © 2013 by Allison Sojka
Cover and Internal Design © 2013 by Allison Sojka

ISBN 13: 978-1490944968
ISBN 10: 1490944966
NoWorriesWhale@gmail.com
P.O.BOX 540416 • Omaha, Nebraska • 68154

Table of Contents:

No Worries Whale

[a book of ocean poems]

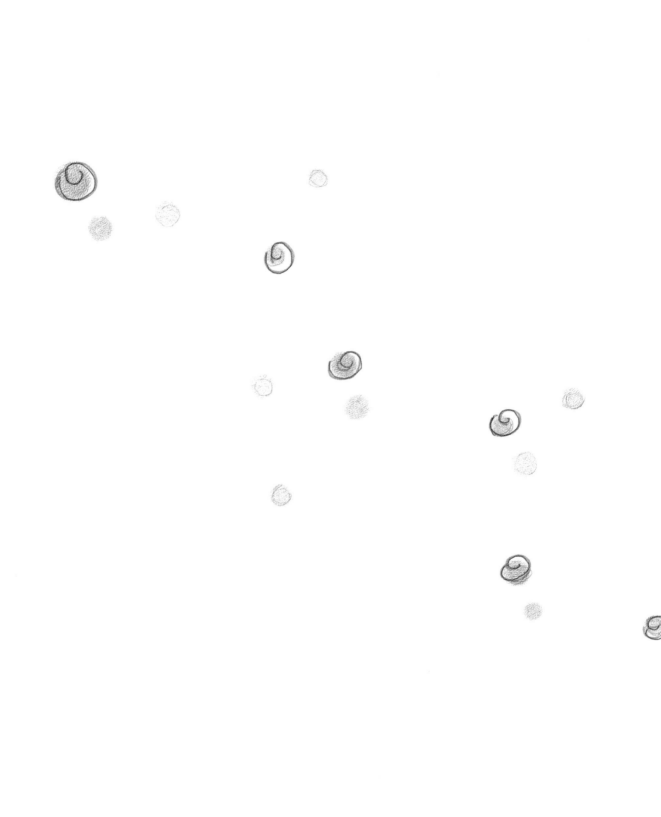

Discovering the Deep

If you ask a scientist of which we could learn more
They'd say we know the moon better than the ocean floor
More people have seen space than the deepest bed of sea
For the depths of the ocean aren't explored so easily
The lowest layers of water are far below the beach
Way down where the sun's rays could never reach
This thick black darkness hides a habitat unknown
A place that many creatures have come to call their home
We know that they are down there, yet cannot name them all
Whatever is at the bottom, whoever swims and crawls
We cannot go and meet them, for the pressure will increase
The farther we swim down the more the water starts to squeeze
We need special tools to explore the ocean floor
Maybe you'll invent something, so someday we'll know more

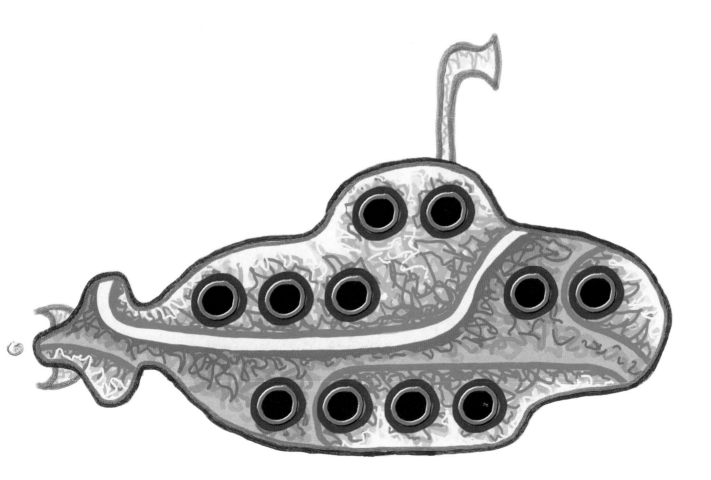

Touring Turtle

Thomas the touring turtle
Born on a Florida beach
Set off to find his mother
Who was somewhere out of reach
He loved the sites he saw
Within the ocean bed
So much he took a detour
And kept on traveling instead
Using the Earth's magnetic field
To navigate his path
How far he'd go he'd never know
Turtles don't do math
He hopped onto a current
Called the North Atlantic Gyre
Cruising east on the Atlantic
Taking five years to admire
He saw so many places
Getting stamps at every one
His shell was fully covered
By the time the trip was done
Although these scenes were magical
Upon the ocean floor
Thomas hadn't found
What he was really looking for
At the end of his migration
He returned to the shore
Where he came across his mother
And was happy forever more

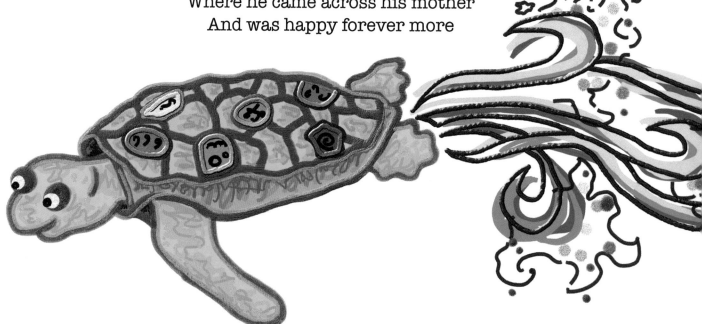

Compulsive Crustacean

Salina the shrimp
Is unnaturally neat
She scrubs all day
With her front feet
She cleans her house
She cleans her friends
She'll clean beyond
This story's end
Her room is spotless
The bed is made
Her socks are folded
And put away
As the day
Turns into night
Salina has cleaned
Everything in sight

Big Dreams, Little Body

Perched on the coral, hardly ever noticed
Lived a pygmy seahorse, named Little Otis
Otis always dreamed of being big and tall
This seahorse was tired of being so small
He wanted to explore and swim the open seas
But his friends would say, "Little Otis, please!
The ocean out there is filled with strangers
Stay here on the coral, away from the dangers."
If only he were bigger than a bitty grain of rice
He'd leave his humble home without thinking twice
For from his view the sea seemed fantastic
Finally one day, Otis did something drastic
Tired of waiting, wishing to be big
He uncurled his tail from his cozy coral sprig
Setting out to discover his watery world
With hopes held high and gray tail curled
Wanting big things even though he was small
He'd never reach his dreams not trying at all

Icefish Playground

Deep in the Antarctic, near the southern pole
Lies a frozen playground in a sea of cold
A place too frosty for you and me
This paradise can be -2 degrees C
A wintery world weaved with whites and blues
Filled with funny fish you can see right through
Fish with no color and even no scales
Just see-through fins and see-through tails
They're hard to see with their clear physique
While playing games of hide and seek
Ducking by icebergs, beneath snow slides
It's difficult to find these fish when they hide
Slipping behind swings as they swim
Then racing around icicle jungle gyms
Playing all day in their freezing habitat
Without anybody knowing where they're at

If only we could play hide and seek like that!

Sea Sway Ballet

A furry looking creature wriggles all around
Searching for a spot to nestle in the ground
He shuffles mud and sands on the ocean base
Until he comes across just the perfect place
Using his tiny tube feet, he starts to dig
This hairy sea cucumber's going to put on a jig
And when he is fixed to the ocean floor
He does something you've never seen before
His body transforms to show a whole new feature
Out pop tentacles from this amazing sea creature
Dazzling little arms like bushy branches
Wave to show you his beautiful dances
They swirl and they swoop as he does the ballet
Eating from the arms, all the while they sway
Just as suddenly as his tentacles popped out
He puts them away, because he's all tired out
As he bids goodnight, we know without a doubt
This hairy sea cucumber's worth talking about

A Plankton Piece

Plankton are plants and animals
Plankton are quite small
You'd have to use a microscope
To see most plankton at all
Some float around in water
Or live upon the floor
Although microscopic
They're too important to ignore
They help the carbon cycle,
They feed the fish and whales,
Many are bacteria
And some have a tail
Some glow in the dark
Some you see right through
They're amazing little creatures
Invisible to me and you

Seaway Circus

Come one, come all
There's no need to fuss!
There's room for you all
At Seaway Circus!

Yes, come find a seat
You're in for a treat
Settle in, settle down
Get something to eat
There's plankton pudding
And algae ice cream
We'll start in a minute
Get ready to scream
The blue-ringed octopus
Will be leading the show
He's the one with the hat
In the ring down below
We'll have dancers and jugglers
And elephant fish
Stay where you're at
So you don't get squished
And after the elephant fish
Have performed
We'll give you something
To get your hearts warmed
The flamefish throwers
Are the hottest things yet
When their act is over
You're sure to have sweat
Following them
We'll cool you down
With seahorses dancing
Alongside the clowns
Then the acro-batfish
Will amaze overhead
They'll tightrope walk
On a seaweed thread

They'll teeter and totter
Until they give in
And leap to the floor
To be caught by the fins
With help from the flying fish
On the trapeze
Who glide and flip through
The water with ease
And when we are through
With this aerial act
The world's strongest manta
Is sure to attract
He will lift things of
Unbelievable weights
And if that doesn't get
Blowfish to inflate
Then the swordfish swallowers
Are likely to keep
You clutching your scales
At the edge of your seat
Finally, we'll present
Last but not least
The lionfish tamer
And his venomous beasts

It's stupendous, amazing
And state of the art!
Hold on to your fins
It's going to start!

It's Big...and It's Blue...

Larger than an elephant
Or any dinosaur
The blue whale is much bigger
Than any animal before
The biggest in water,
On land or in air
Just his heart alone
Is the size of a polar bear
Although he's too enormous
To fit inside this book
He persuaded us to let him
Peek in and take a look

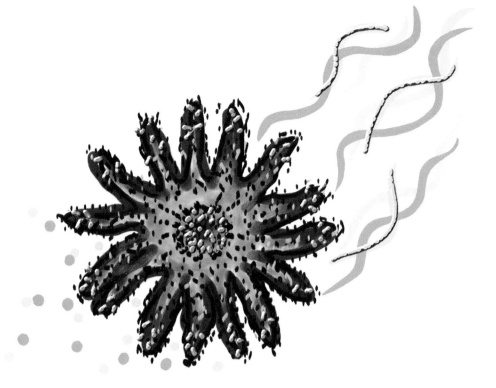

Mealtime Madness

The sunflower sea star
The largest star you'll meet
Has the strangest manners
If you watch her eat
She runs to the table with
Fifteen thousand tube feet
Running over everybody
On the way to her seat
Using twenty arms
Not a fork to eat her treats
Swallowing food whole
Never using teeth
No one's ever told her
Spitting isn't neat
She spits out her stomach
Every time she eats
It helps her digest food
If it's too big of a treat
Then she puts it back in place
When the meal is complete
I wouldn't say
That her manners are sweet
Would you invite her to
Your house to eat?

The Coy Christmas Tree Worms

In almost every ocean
Beneath the sharks and whales
Is a fantastical forest
The kind found in fairy tales
A watery woodland unlike
Any wilderness you've seen
There are trees of every color
In this grove of evergreens
Spirals of red and yellow
With swirls of pink and blue
They come in orange and white
Green and purple too
Each and every tree
Has a twin at its side
Feathery conifers dancing
On the coral with the tide
Their jig is rather catchy
It makes you want to dance
But if you get too close
You'll never get the chance

Every tree will vanish
Faster than you blink
For this magical forest
Isn't exactly what you think
It isn't really filled
With colorful dancing ferns
Beneath each set of trees
Is a tiny burrowed worm
These worms all dance in secret
With no one else around
And if they sense you're watching
They'll pop into the ground
So, in case you're not too sneaky
But would like to take a look
We put this wormy woodland
Inside your ocean book!

Aquatic Academy

Schools of fish, swim in a bunch
Just like you they have recess and lunch
There are schools of tuna, squid and herring
Swimming in shapes in their fishy pairings
They move the same speed, go the same way
And when they're done learning they go home to play

Cookie Cutter Clark

There is a shark whose name is Clark
Who loves to bake confections
He likes to bake cookies and cakes
He has the best selection
All the while, his charming smile's
The only tool he keeps
They help make the things he bakes
And even help him eat
He uses his jaws to bake because
They make the perfect shape
His rounded mouth cuts circles out
It never makes mistakes
He can cook without a book
And even in the dark
That's why he's named and even famed
The cookie cutter shark

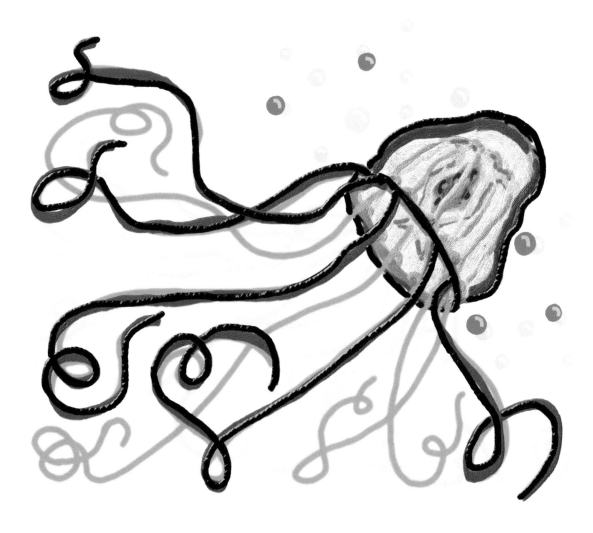

The Eternal Jelly
-Turritopsis Nutricula-

Immortal is to live forever
Which no human has ever done
But we came across a creature
Who's comparable to none
It's thought to last much longer
Than any people do
Who is it do you wonder
That we give this credit to?
A tiny little jelly
No bigger than a pea
Who lives among the plankton
At the bottom of the sea
Its name is hard to say
Its body is hard to see
But this itty bitty creature
May live infinitely

Mediev-Eel Moray

Once upon a time
In a castle on the reef
Locked high in a tower
And guarded by a thief
A damselfish in distress
Waiting to be saved
While a dragon moray eel
Guarded nearby from a cave
The waters to her rescue
Were dangerous at best
No fish who tried to save her
Came closer than the next
For the dragon eel lay waiting
With a mouth of razor teeth
Sniffing out intruders
With the horns he used to breathe
Watching over his treasures
Long lost to the sea
Anything that caught his eye
He'd say was meant for thee
So, he kept the lovely damselfish
Within the tower peak
For her beauty was unmatched
By any you would meet
Her scales were dazzling sapphires
But even sweeter to behold
Were the fins that swayed behind her
Painted all in gold
This is why he took her
And kept her as his treasure
To him she was a gem
For him to have forever
Her story was a sad one
That spread across the sea
Until it fell upon
A courageous knight goby

Who better to save her
Than this fish of silvery white
A fish as brave as him
Who happened to be a knight
He set off to save this damsel
Upon his trusty steed
Racing on his seahorse
To help the fish in need
They traveled far to find her
Within the ocean bed
And when they came upon her
In the tower overhead

The dragon eel was guarding
The damselfish he kept
So, the knight goby lay waiting
Until the dragon slept
He hid among the seaweed
Where his steed and he would blend
Until the dragon slumbered
To save their lady friend
And when the eel was drowsy
He went into his cave
The knight goby and seahorse
Swam swiftly through the waves
Thus, rescuing the damselfish
Never taking hits
Fighting wasn't needed
Instead they fought with wits

Sea Spray Speedway

When the flags go down
These fish hit the track
They never back down
And never hold back
The fastest racers
Known to the ocean
These sailfish cause
Quite a commotion
They move through the sea
At a pace that astounds
But these speedsters
Don't make engine sounds
They don't use cars
To cross finish lines
Just fins, tails
And sails down their spines
That's all they need
When they go to compete
For they can't drive cars
They don't have feet

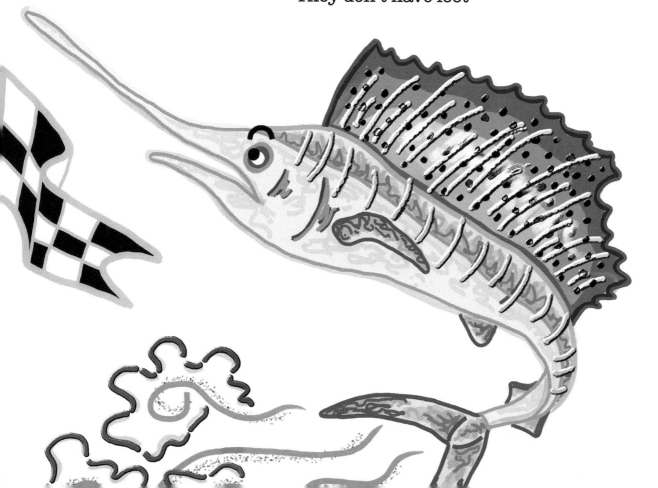

Blobby

This fish has no muscles
He's only a glob
A gelatinous fish
Who calls himself Blob
He has a blob for a head,
A blob for a nose
And if he had any
He'd have blobs for toes
Everything about
The blob fish is blobby
Being a blob
Is his favorite hobby
Blob doesn't do much
So there's not much to say
He just bobs in the ocean
And blobs life away

Mimic Magic

Mimic Octopus
A magician under the sea
Wakes up each morning
And decides who to be
You wouldn't recognize him
If he swam by
He changes his shape
In the blink of an eye
Mimic may act
As a shrimp or a fish
He transforms to a snake
Or a crab with a swish
He swims in the open,
Burrows the ground,
Hovers the bottom
And even runs around
Mimic becomes anything
By changing his shape
He's a mystic magician
With no need for a cape
His shape-shifting act
Is performed without spells
How does he do it?
A magician never tells

Napoleon the Narwhal

The Arctic's to the north
On a globe, above us all
It's just the sort of place
You'll find Napoleon Narwhal
He lives in the Arctic
In fact, he never leaves
If you wander that far north
You will spot him there with ease
He travels with his friends
A group he calls his pod
His favorite meals are halibut,
Squid, shrimp and cod
He's black, white and speckled
And bigger than you'd assume
If you take him home
He won't fit inside your room
He's a wondrous whale
To tell the truth
Right above his eyes
Napoleon has a tooth
Not just any tooth
A twisty spirally horn
That makes this lovable whale
Resemble a unicorn
So, if you visit the Arctic
Or live there like some do
Say hello to Napoleon
He might whistle back at you!

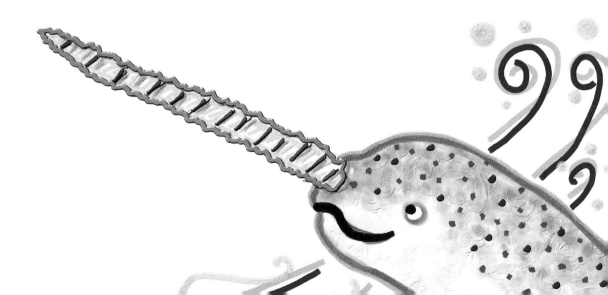

Coral St-Arrgh Cove

Long, long ago
Near an island not too far
A mighty ship sailed
With the name Coral Star
It roamed the seven seas
With pirates on its deck
Until it met an awful fate
Those pirates had a wreck
The Coral Star's sailing days
Ended with its sink
Or so we landlubbers
Always tend to think
But though we cannot see it
Doesn't mean it's done
For on the ocean floor below
Its story had just begun...

Bandit, a parrotfish
Lived upon the reef
Always dreaming of pirate life
Living as a thief
Bandit found the Coral Star,
Made it his new roost
And shared it with a pilot fish
Oddly nicknamed Goose
Bandit, the captain
Ordered all the crew
With Goose the only other
In their crew of merely two
Goose was the navigator
As he was a pilot fish
Now, their buccaneering dreams
No longer just a wish
Pillaging for treasure
Mostly finding food
Living the lives of pirates
They were rough, tough, and rude

Swimming and talking like pirates
And laughing like them too
Saying "Aargh!" and "Har!" and "Matey!"
Just as pirates do
Bandit and Goose were scallywags
Ignoring manners and such
The other fish all stayed away
They didn't like that much
"The pirate's life is a lonely life,"
The two would always say
They liked each other far too much
To care less, anyway
So, though we like to think
Sinking was its end
The Coral Star forever lives
Among these two fish friends

...Think about that next time
You're throwing things away
For much like the Coral Star
Trash won't just go away

Recycle Matey!

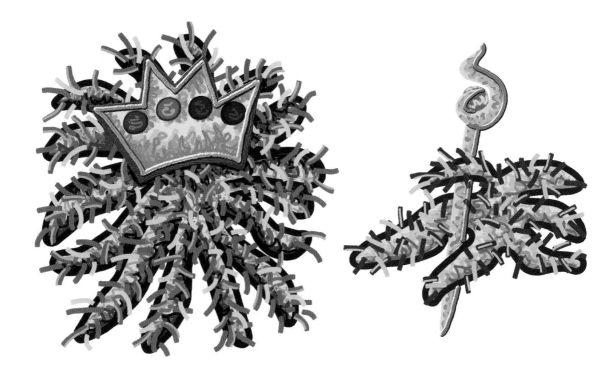

King of the Echinoderms

Leopold the starfish
Wore a crown of thorns
He longed to be the king
From the day he was born
Using many tube feet
Below his star-like frame
He crawled along the ocean floor
Seeking out his fame
One day he found a reef
Unlike any he had known
He claimed this coral kingdom
And made it his new home
But royal life was not
What he thought at all
He wanted kingly parties
He wanted royal balls
So, he put to work a plan
To grow his mighty throne
For every leg a starfish loses
Turns into a clone
He appointed one advisor,
One jester and one queen
A bigger royal party
No one had ever seen

Multiplied by many
They took over the reef
Destroying homes of others
Because coral's all they'd eat
Who knew all the damage
These stars could cause together?
Imagine if they worked instead
To leave their world better

Lucy's Light

Lucy lives in the darkest part of the sea
She goes fishing below three thousand feet
Carrying a pole on her dorsal spine
She lights her world with a luminous shine
Her lure gets brighter with every frown
For you can't let the darkness keep you down
So, if things in your life don't seem so bright
Do like the anglerfish, bring your own light
No amount of darkness can hide your spark
When you light the world with the love in your heart

What A Fishy Farm

A forever rolling
Watery plot
Just below
The fishermen's knot
Acreages of things
So unique
An undersea farmland
So to speak
Where sea cows graze
Along the coast
Eating the grass
They love the most
Where color changing
Goatfish stray
Searching for food
In meadowy bays

Roosterfish strut
Around the ocean bed
Combs standing tall
On top of their heads
Bull sharks that
Are large and stout
Show off their muscles
And their snouts
But the cutest creatures
We just can't miss
Are sea pigs rolling
In the muddy abyss
Seahorses, goosefish
Creatures galore
Living on the farm
Off the ocean shore

Perhaps it's a stretch
A sea weedy plantation
But anything's possible
With your imagination!

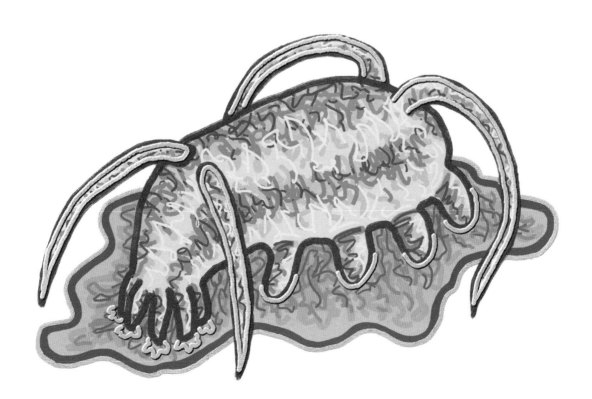

Introverted Archibald

Two fins, a mantle,
A single head,
Eight arms and two tentacles
To fit in his bed
In the ocean depths
Archibald resides
For here, from the other
Fish he can hide
Endowed with suckers
And mid-arm hooks
Other fish give this
Giant squid funny looks
No one treats him
Like he quite fits in
Because he's a rather
Rare specimen
But I rather like him
He's worth a peek
What makes him different
Makes him unique!
For it's not like he
Can be somebody else
Who would he be
If not himself?

Hums of the Humpback

There is a mammal
The humpback whale
If you weighed him
He'd break your scale
He's fifty feet long,
Eighty thousand pounds
This jumbo whale
Makes beautiful sounds
He swims in the ocean
Jollying along
All the while
Singing magical songs
And before people
Filled up the ocean
With ships, noise
And lots of commotion
The song of the whale
Traveled easily forth
From the pole in the south
To the pole in the north
From the top of the Earth
All the way back down
He once was the whale
Heard world round

Hug Me Crabby

The Japanese spider crab
Seems rather odd
This giant critter
The largest arthropod
His crabby appearance
May cause you alarm
With eight long legs
And two feeding arms
Covered in thorns
That are a bit hairy
With claws on his arms
Both big and scary
His body is little
With legs so atrocious
But the spider crab
Is hardly ferocious
He may be a crab
That looks like a bug
But all that he wants
Is someone to hug
He is peaceful, friendly
And really a lover
So, just like a book
Don't judge a crab by his cover

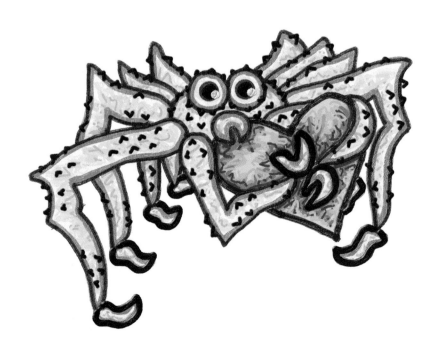

Slumbers of the Sleeper Shark

Sammy the sleeper shark
Loves to take naps
However, he is
An unfortunate chap
There is no need
For counting sheep
When he accidently
Falls asleep
Trying to eat
A giant squid
He fell asleep
And never did

Oh dear, I'm kidding
Forget that remark
That's not at all why
He's called sleeper shark!

...What, you want the answer?
Well go find out
That's what discovering's
All about!

Helping Handfish

Hamlet the handfish
Was very greedy
Grabby, impatient
And incredibly needy
He wanted everything
Not caring about others
Taking anything from anyone
Even his brothers
But no matter how much
He wanted this stuff
He was never happy
There was never enough
One day Hamlet met
A witch flounder fish
Who said that she would
Grant him any wish
But in return he needed
To help somebody else
Only then would he get
A wish for himself

Hamlet didn't want
To help other fishes
He wanted everything
Including more wishes
While he was throwing
A fit about this
Along came a very
Distraught little fish
Her bottle stuck tight
With a message inside
That she couldn't open
Though she twisted and tried
Then the handfish said
"Perhaps I could try
I can open it
There's no need to cry
I'm the only fish
With hands in the sea
Who better to open
This bottle than me?"
So, he took the bottle
To help the fish
Knowing for sure
This would earn his wish
As he helped her
A surprise of his own!
His heart had a feeling
To him unknown
The fish was so happy
And grateful for help
That Hamlet the handfish
Felt happy himself
He didn't need wishes
Or things from others
What made him happy
Was helping another
So, when the witch asked
What he wanted for himself
Hamlet said he'd rather
Give than get help

Calamity Crab

What exactly is this happy crab doing
With all eight feet tapping and shoeing?
Dancing along with the clammy choir
Like there's ants in his pants or his shoes are on fire
But that's not it, for I hear no alarms
Wait, are those puppets on his feeding arms?
His sideways dancing is going so fast
I'm surprised at this speed his shell hasn't cracked!
Perhaps he won't care if his shell or legs bolt
He'll grow new ones every time that he molts

So, Mr. Crab, why are you in this state?
Oh isn't that nice, you're attracting a mate
Lady crabs like it when you make all this noise?
And show off your claws covered with toys?
They like when your feet clip and they clop?
Well then by all means, keep going, don't stop!

The Clown with a Frown

Bubbles the clownfish wears a wig
And a polka dot dress two sizes too big
She juggles and sings to try and amuse
Telling jokes that often leave others confused
Trying to live up to her clownfish name
That tells everyone else that life is a game
Her three white stripes mark her as a clown
So, she'll spend her whole life clowning around
Juggling, joking and singing off key
Until she goes home to her sea anemone
Where she'll crawl into her tentacle bed
Wishing she had another name instead
It's hard finding jokes to tell every day
And juggling with fins is tough, anyway

Bubbles just wants to be herself
So, she's chosen to stop being somebody else
If others don't like it, well that's too bad
This clownfish grew tired of being so sad
No one should tell you who to be
Just be yourself and live happily

Coral Reef

We spend so much time telling
About the life in this space
But it's important to know
The coral reef's more than a place
It's made of many animals
That once were pretty small
They attached themselves to rocks
And began to stretch and sprawl
It took a long, long time
For these little polyps to grow
Some reefs started growing
Millions of years ago
And though less than one percent
Of oceans have these features
The coral reef is home
To almost one fourth of its creatures
Without the coral's support
These animals will go extinct
So, remember that the reef
Is more important than you think
When we contaminate the water
And pollute the Earth
It's the corals and animals
Of the oceans who get hurt
So, if you love the ocean
And marine life that brave it
Reduce, reuse, recycle
It's the only way to save it

Sea Butterfly

Imagine your feet turning into wings
Would they take you places? Show you things?

For a little snail living under the sea
This is more than mere thought or fantasy
His foot was so tired from trekking the floor
It decided to change into something much more
And what happens when your foot's a device for flight?
You fly upside down, not upside right!
He hangs by his foot, now two flappy things
That sail through the sea like two tiny wings
And if he gets hungry along his travels
A mucus web, he slowly unravels
It drapes down beneath him...or is it above?
And catches the planktonic food that he loves
If anyone disturbs him, he'll drop his net
And glide away from whatever the threat
He's a graceful creature the size of a bean
That's accomplished every kid's flying dream

A Great White Smile

Reggie the shark had three thousand teeth
But only one in his mouth was sweet
One day, a row of his teeth really hurt
He tried to feel better by eating dessert
Each snack he ate made Reggie more troubled
For the pain in his mouth had nearly doubled
Reggie decided to go to the dentist
Who better to see than a dental hygienist?
He made an appointment close to the reef
For the dentist to see him and fix his hurt teeth
When the dentist came in to talk to Reggie
He asked if he brushed and ate his veggies
Reggie looked down at his fins and blushed
He didn't eat veggies and barely brushed
The dentist just smiled, for he knew the truth
Reggie the shark had a giant sweet tooth
He said to eat better and brush his teeth right
Now Reggie's a happy and healthy Great White

Sea Snakes

More toxic than cobras
Or their friends on land
Hissing through the ocean
Wearing little black bands
Spearing out forked tongues
Using them to smell
Searching for some fish
Or food with a shell
Slinking in shadows
Slithering the depths
Hiding in the shallows
Only surfacing for breaths
Their fangs are rather tiny
But pack quite a punch
However, they won't hurt you
Unless you're their lunch

Captivating Cuttlefish

Chloe the cuttlefish
An ocean work of art
Is the sweetest creature
A mollusk with three hearts
All the more to love with
Yet, her body holds much more
A brain that is much bigger
Than her shape gives credit for
With her wits she's able
To wear her hearts upon her sleeve
Her color changes with her mood
In seconds she can weave
Beautiful patterns on her skin
That dance across her back
In brilliant reds and yellows,
Golds, greens and blacks
She is the queen of camouflage
With her color changing act
Fading into scenery
Painted perfectly to match
Chloe glides with the waves
Fins flowing at her sides
And there's no doubt she is
A masterpiece among the tides

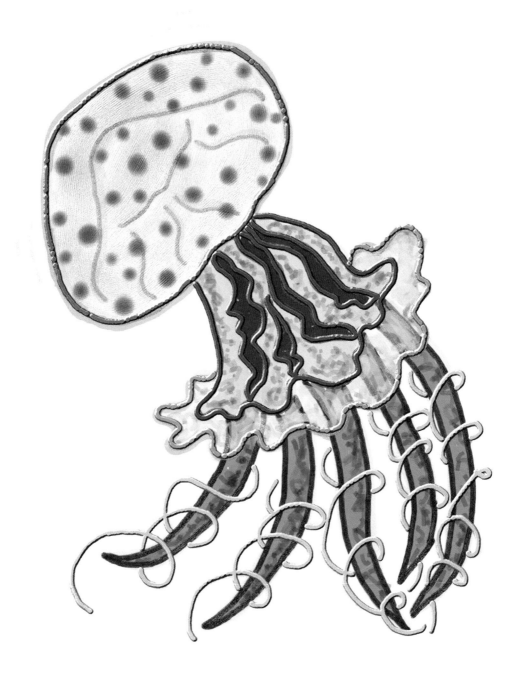

Mixed up Medusas

Did you know jellyfish aren't made of jelly?
And they don't have hearts inside their bellies?
Here's a mind-blowing fact, if you wish
Jellyfish are not even fish!
Gelatinous Zooplankton are better words
Though kind of big and hardly heard
But this sort of thing, jellies can't explain
Mostly because jellyfish have no brains!
So really, you can call them whatever you wish
There is no arguing with jellyfish

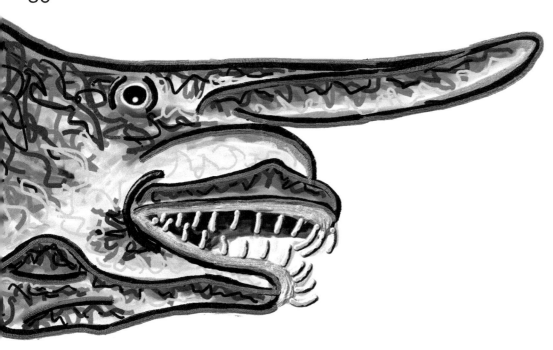

Marine Halloween

There is a place
Below the tides
Where hoards of fish
All live and hide
They're frightening fish
Like Halloween
Beneath the waters
They go unseen
When other fish
Have gone to sleep
At night, they all
Come out to creep
Goblin sharks
So full of guile
Have pointed noses
Above their smiles
At dark
Vampire crabs arise
With purple shells
And big orange eyes
Along with flounders
Known as witches
A charming label
For these fishes

Flatfish witches
No brooms to ride
With both their eyes
On one side
Their catfish howl
In the direction of
Moonfish looming
In the sea above
As ghost shrimp spook
Beneath the rest
Cleaning up
Their monstrous mess
So, if you're up
For a scary sight
Visit the ocean
Depths at night
For we like to think
That monsters creep
Inside our closets
When we sleep
But the truth is not
So hard to keep
They live under
The ocean deep
And they'll stay scary
Until we know
More about
The sea below
For we fear the things
We can't explain
So, get out there
And fill your brain

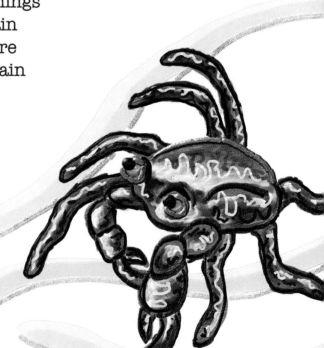

Crooning Clam
-Tune: "Baa Baa Black Sheep"-

[Verse 1]

Giant clam, giant clam
How do you eat?
I catch food
With no hands or feet

I eat algae
Eat it all day
I open up my shell
As it floats my way

Giant clam, giant clam
How do you eat?
I catch food
With no hands or feet

[Verse 2]

Giant clam, giant clam
How big can you grow?
Sometimes five hundred
Pounds or so

I'm the biggest mollusk
In the sea
No other clam
Is as big as me

Giant clam, giant clam
How big can you grow?
Sometimes five hundred
Pounds or so

[Verse 3]

Giant clam, giant clam
Where do you sleep?
Here in the ocean
Sixty feet deep

I snuggle in the sand
And snore in my shell
Here I'm safe
And I sleep so well

Giant clam, giant clam
Where do you sleep?
Here in the ocean
Sixty feet deep

Love the Lobster

If I asked, "What is a lobster?"
Would you say something you ate?
Well, the lobster was a living thing
Before it topped your plate
This bright and colorful dish
Once was so much more
Living among the rocks and grass
Along the ocean floor
An impressive crustacean, once
With four antennas used to smell,
Ten little legs to walk on
And a beautifully colored shell
And every time he grew too big
To wear his shell-like skin
He would take it off and wait
For a new shell to grow in
This arthropod swam backwards
Flicking the fins on his tail
Once upon a time this lobster
Lived in the world of whales
So, before you use your knife and fork
Follow this rule of thumb:
Always find out what you're eating
And know where your food comes from
For if we gobble up all the lobster
And they are overfished
There won't be any lobsters left
For the oceans or a dish

Scanning the Skies

Stella has her eyes
Set on the stars
Looking up, looking out
Gazing towards Mars
This Barreleye fish
Scans the way to the skies
Taking it in
With her telescope eyes
For the universe is like
A book unread
That she ponders inside
Her see-through head

And her eyes are where
Do you suppose?
They're the little green barrels
Behind her nose!

Silky Shark Spells

If ever there lived
A fairy godmother of the sea
Perhaps we would choose
The shark called Silky
She wears her silver skin
Like a smooth satin cape
Sweeping through the ocean
As she migrates
With her super hearing
She travels around
Finding fish in need
Of magic or a gown
Does she have a wand
To cast twinkling spells?
Does her magic stop
When the clock strikes twelve?
Wait, do fish have clocks?
I don't know, do you?
Can you imagine sharks
Singing Bibbidi-Bobbidi-Boo?
Perhaps she is the fish
Who will make your dreams come true
...Don't ask if you're a tuna
She just might eat you!

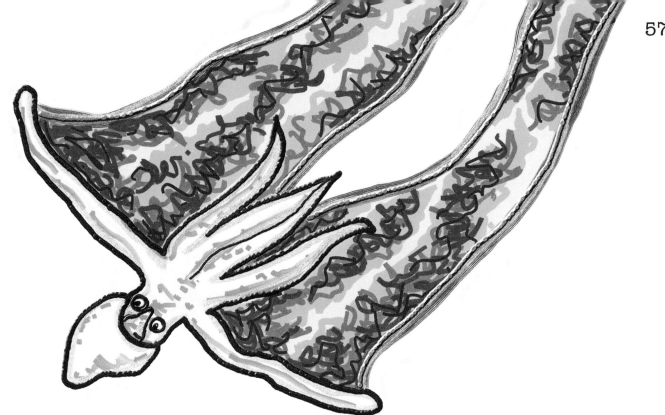

Superhero of the Seas

Beans the blanket octopus
Brings her blanky everywhere
Colored red and yellow
She cuddles it with care
For unlike other octopi
She carries no ink sac
Instead Beans has her blanket
She wears upon her back
This blanket keeps her safe
Even when she is afraid
She'll unfurl it from her arms
Below her it cascades
Surrounded by open ocean
It gives Beans a bigger shape
Just like a superhero
It trails behind her like a cape
It protects her from the ruffians
Lurking in the deep
And when it's time for bed
It snuggles this superhero to sleep

Cock-A-Doodle-Doo

Knock, knock
Who's there?
Cock-a-doodle
Who?

That's the roosterfish crowing
From California to Peru
But his squawk is not as sharp
As his seven-spined back
Standing tall upon his top
Decked out in silvery black
And when his job is done
His comb-like fins retract
Returning to the pocket
Where he keeps them packed

Catfish Clutter

This catfish loves
His litter box
But not the kind
With little rocks
His litter box is
His home, you see
The watery deep
Filled with debris
It's littered because
It's filled with junk
Like plastic bags
And trash that sunk
Because someone, somewhere
Didn't know
The ocean's where
Their garbage goes
So, when he feeds
From the floor
His barbel whiskers
Get kind of sore
From bumping and bouncing
Off of waste
That doesn't belong here
In this space

A Brave Tail

Polly the pufferfish
Was scared of anything at all
For her world was very big
While she was very small
Polly was scared of bubbles,
Terrified of the dark,
Afraid of getting lost
Or perhaps meeting sharks
With all her silly worries
You'd think she'd just stay home
But puffer fish are curious
Polly liked to roam
One day she lost her way
And met a lizardfish
Who splashed with joy to see her
For she was his favorite dish
Polly tried to run
But her fins wouldn't sway
Her scale-less body wasn't made
To help her run away
The lizardfish raced toward her
He tried to take a bite
Polly gulped a great big gulp
Then swelled up twice her size!

Her tiny spiny body
Miraculously fattened
She grew a bit braver
As this inflation happened
With her new size and courage
The lizard gave up soon
For his mouth would never fit
Around a spiky fish balloon
And as he swam away
Polly Puffer was elated
Who knew I was so brave?
She thought, as she deflated

If Polly could do this
What else can she do?
She can change the world
Guess what? So can you!

Pucker Kiss Angelfish

There's no such thing as too many kisses
Just go ask the angelfishes

Aqua Zoo

We the plankton keepers
Welcome you to Aqua Zoo
Come explore this habitat
And meet our wild crew!
Meet lion's mane jellies
With red and orange features
Hundreds of tentacles
The largest of our creatures
There are zebra seahorses
Striped white and black
With babies all nestled
In their father's pouch sack
Go left at the kelp beds
To meet leopard sharks
Playing in schools
With leopard spotted marks
Find tiger rockfish
One hundred years old
With bright pink lips
And stripes so bold
Go see the trunks
On our elephant seals
And make silly faces
With monkey face eels
Nothing is better
Than a day at our zoo
So, come line up
And learn something new!

tiger rockfish

leopard sharks

zebra seahorses

monkey face eels

elephant seals

Anchovy Antics

Hello, Dr. Doctorfish
It's me, Anchovy Claire
Here to tell you of
My fishy nightmare
Each night I fall asleep
In my muddy salty bed
Then a strange dream
Rolls around inside my head
First, I'm in my mud
Then, it turns to cheese?
I know I've left the water
I'm a few hundred degrees
I'm not always alone
Sometimes I'm next to Lisa
So, tell me Dr. DoctorFish
Have you ever heard of pizza?

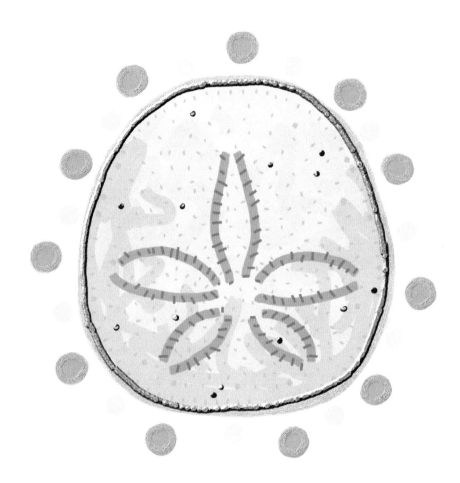

This Money is Funny

I found a sand dollar
While walking the shore
I pondered to myself
What do fish need money for?
I'm curious and wondering
And kind of amused
Thinking up ways
This money was used

Are they shopping down there
When we aren't looking?
Are there grocery stores?
If so, are they cooking?
Maybe this is valuable?
Perhaps I'm now rich!
Then again, perhaps not
Is there something I've missed?
I'm asking these questions
This isn't quite working
I'm off on a mission
I've found myself searching
Looking at pictures
Hunting in books
To discover the secrets
Are there undersea cooks?
Finally, an answer
It turns my brain to gelatin!
A sand dollar isn't money
It's only a skeleton!
There aren't any stores?
No chefs or sea merchants?
These are only the bones
Of little sea urchins?
I admit I'm quite gloomy
I didn't get rich
I didn't uncover
The secret life of fish
Until I realize
It's better than I wished
I'm the finder of bones
I'm an archaeologist!

Picasso Fish

Picasso Fish lived in a sea of black and white
A world so different from his dreams at night
He imagined a world painted in rainbow hues
Of reds and golds, greens and blues
But when he looked at the sea the colors faded
To the black and white way his world was shaded
So, he decided the world should open their eyes
And think outside their black and white lives
He painted his blacks with streaks of blue
And gave his white lips some yellow too
For before he could change how the world felt
He had to start by changing himself
The world has problems that need to be fixed
So, take the advice of Picasso Fish
The colors are out there waiting to mix
Get out your paintbrush and paint your lips
Then when you're done painting your face
Go paint the world a better place

Delighting in Dolphins

Meet a cetacean that surfs the waves
And travels through the watery bays
We know she's a mammal, she has a spout
That holds her breath and blows it out
Her blowhole does more than respiration
It helps her blow bubble ring formations!
She'll spin and pop them as she plays
Playing is how she spends her days
But other than fun she's really smart
As good with her brains as with her heart
She'll find some squid or a hiding crustacean
Using something called echolocation
Where she clicks and whistles waves of sound
That echo back from off the ground
Sending a message like an X-ray
That tells her where to find her prey
She uses sound, not sight or smell
She's pretty amazing if you can't tell
It's said, she's the smartest in the sea
Maybe smarter than you and me

Counting Sea Shapes

One oval butterflyfish
Swimming in the dark
Two diamond squids
Exercising their three hearts
Four red sea stars
Waving all five arms
Six rectangle triggerfish
With color changing charms
Seven square crabs
Run with eight tiny feet
While nine triangle crabs
Eat ten sponges for a treat

Monstrous Mambo

The vampire squid lives deep in the dark
His name is scary, so we'll call him Mark
His cloak of webbing fits like a cape
That covers his black gelatinous shape
His bat-like fins flap on his mantle
Above red eyes blazing like candles
But he's much more charming than he is frightful
He only lives in the dark, for he finds it delightful
There he can dance with his glowing blue feet
That wiggle below his cape in the deep
He is a bit different, but fun all the same
Just give him a chance, for what's in a name?

Stop That Copy-Cat

Stop copying me...
Hey! Would you cut it out?
You repeat every word
That comes out of my mouth!
Parrotfish, parrotfish
Please go away
You're talking and talking
You've ruined my day
You're scraping my ears
Like you do to the corals
My head's had enough
Go munch on your florals!

Oh, you parrot fish
You're all the same
Jibbering and jabbering
The corals to grains
My brain feels eroded
I feel bad for the reef
You're tearing it down
With unstoppable teeth
Bioeroding the sponges
You've got that down pat
Wait just a minute
You didn't know that?
Funny, now I think
I'm glad we're talking
You should sit down
You might find this shocking
Bioerosion is bad
For the oceans, dude!
It's what parrotfish do
When looking for food
Chewing corals to sand
While eating your lunch
You're destroying the reef
Every time you munch
What's that you say?
You didn't know that before?
Perhaps you were talking
Too loud to ignore
Maybe you didn't hear
What others would say
When your mouth was moving
And moving all day
Tomorrow try listening
I bet you'll learn more
If your ears work harder
Than your mouth did before

Sea Symphony

Moonlight dances on the waves
Music streams below
Waltzes play on every crest
Tumbling toward the coast
These nautical notes sail
From the ocean floor
Composed by a symphony
Of musician fish galore
Trumpet fish trumpeting
Through their tubular snouts
Accompanied by horn sharks
Piping octaves out

Drum fish thumping
On their hollow bellies
Then drumming and thudding
On top of the jellies
Atlantic guitarfish
Strumming their scales
Among musicians
In white ties and tails
Harp seals who traveled
From the Arctic to play
Pluck at their strings
In a harmonic display
Triangle crabs
All chime with the beat
While tapping gently
With eight crabby feet
Then, Wobbegong signals
The end of the song
The final note clapping
With a crash of his gong

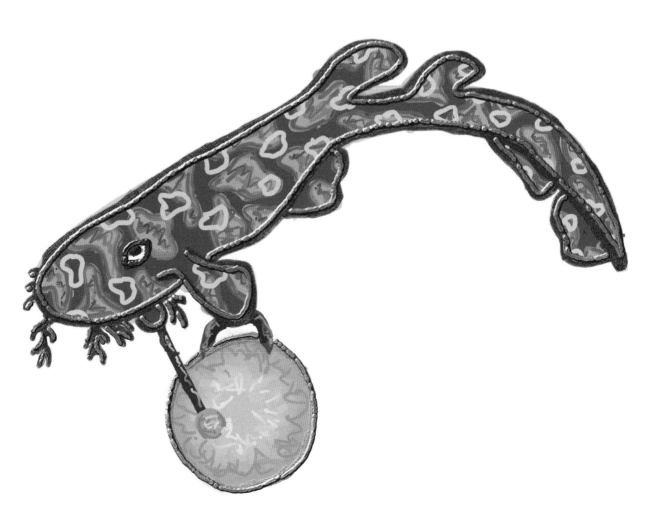

Bloodbelly Comb Jelly

We're about to dive down to the darkest part of sea
To meet a little creature, the bloodbelly comb jelly
He has a tuneful title that ties your tongue in twists
But his stomach's colored red, so it makes sense to call him this
We'll explore and find him, grab your scuba stuff
We're going to the depths to find this diamond in the rough
He lures us with lights, dancing up and down
Waving rows of rainbows lighting up his neon crown
As we swim in closer we see what's really there
Not rows of lights at all just glowing little hairs
These radiant little organs, called cilia, help him travel
Instead of tentacles these frills help him paddle
And though we could spend hours with our balloonish friend
We'll head back to the surface, for all adventures have to end

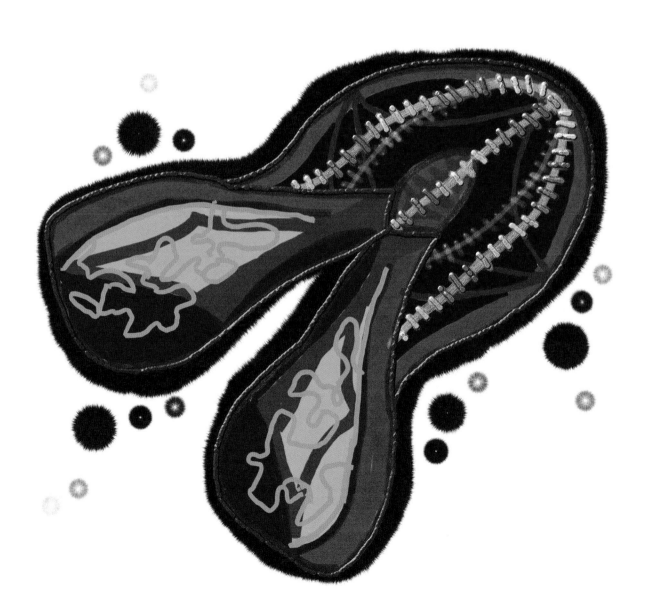

Hearty Pajama Party

You're invited to a party
Here is where to meet:
Off the coast of Africa
Along the rocky reef
We'll be there in the summer
Bring your pj's too
We're partying with catsharks
Wearing jammies just like you
These pajama catsharks
Wear their favorite types
Of grayish colored pj's
Adorned with blackish stripes
Sharks that love sleepovers,
Staying up all night,
Bouncing on the kelp beds
And having seaweed fights
Snacking on their favorites
Lobster and squid stew
They're harmless to us humans
So, this party's safe for you!

You and Me Will Save the Sea

You've decided the ocean
Is a place you like?
Well, conserving it's as easy
As riding your bike
Or walking instead of
Taking the car
Or turning off lights
When you leave where you are
Instead of elevators
Choose stairs if you can
And recycling at home
Would be a good plan

Because how much better
Do you think it would be
If all that trash wasn't
In the dump or the sea?
Not in the ocean
Or littering the beach?
Harming the fish
Or destroying the reefs?
A reusable water bottle
Will reduce the plastic
And the change in this habitat
Will be quite drastic
Then perhaps at the market
Or at the store
Bring reusable bags
To help out even more
And when you are there
Buy food that's organic
So chemicals won't wash
Into the Atlantic
Or better yet try
To grow your own food
It's good for the ocean
And good for you too!
For we all need the ocean
The fishes and you
Your every other breath
Comes from the briny blue
Making simple changes
In your day to day
Makes the world a better place
Tomorrow and today

So, now you're an expert
On conserving the sea
Go share what you know
With everybody!
World change starts at home
And if we work together
We can help the oceans
Stay healthy forever!

Looking for Me?

You can look, but I'm not in a book
I'm somebody no one has seen
Perhaps you think I'm blue or pink
I could be spotted or green
With gills, fins, flippers or skin
Maybe hands or claws?
I could be sweet or have thirty feet
But you won't know because
I'm down so deep where secrets keep
Miles and miles below
And if you don't care for oceans up there
I'm someone you may never know

Pondering Polka Dots

What a handsome stingray
Blue spots upon his top
But where and how would you say
He got his topside spots?
These vibrant dots of vivid blue
How could they just appear?
I couldn't tell an answer true
How did the blue get here?

Using my imagination
I can think up a way or two
And if we work together
We can think up a few
Perhaps he's got a lot of eyes?
Hmm, these blues don't blink
What if squid propelling by
Blotted him with ink, you think?
Maybe he got caught in rain
And forgot his fish umbrella
Can a drizzle of rain maybe explain
Blue splashes on this fella?
Or what if the cookie cutter shark
Thought he was a cake
Had blue sprinkles in a jar
And gave him a few shakes?
Perhaps a passing picasso fish
Saw him taking a nap
And couldn't help but paint
A work of art upon his back
What are your ideas when
You ponder polka dots?
What hypothesis could give
This stingray his blue spots?

Bad Hair Blenny

Ask a yellowfin fringehead
Why he never leaves home
He'll tell you it's because
He lost his favorite comb
Rolling from his shale bed
He refuses to come out
Because his hair's so messy
Sticking up and sticking out
But what adventures can he have
While hiding out in there?
And what fun is living
If you spend your time so scared?
Your greatest journey in life
Is being there for the ride
And you never know who might love
The you hiding inside

Chocolate Chip Sea Stars

Tasty little morsels
Fresh from the ocean oven
Arranged on a sandy sheet
A warm bakers dozen
With a creamy cookie color
And five toasted tips
Topped with tiny cones
Of milk chocolate chips
Adding sweet appeal
To the gravelly floor
Hiding in the sea grass
Near the ocean shore
No star is the same
Each frosted different colors
A favorite food of triggerfish,
Boxfish and puffers
If you see one you will know
They're not the ones we eat
For if you rolled them over
You'd see tons of purple feet!

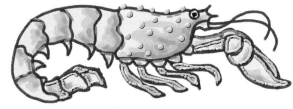

Undersea A to Z

We're on a mission to explore the sea
Off to discover creatures A to Z!

A is for anemone

Barreleye fish for B

C is for cape lobster

Dolphin starts with D

E is for eel

F for flounder witch

Guppy begins with G

H for handfish

I is for icefish

Jellyfish starts with J

K is for krill

L for lamprey

Manatee starts with M

Narwhal with an N

O is an octopus

P for pacific salmon

Q is a quillfish

Rainbowfish starts with R

S is for sea pig

T for tiger shark

U is for urchin

Vampire squid with V

W is for whale shark

X for X-ray fishy

Y is for yellow tang

Zebrafish starts with Z

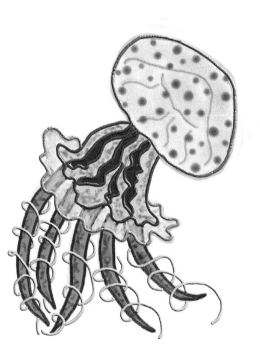

Mission accomplished, hooray for you and me!
We found the Alphabet under the sea!

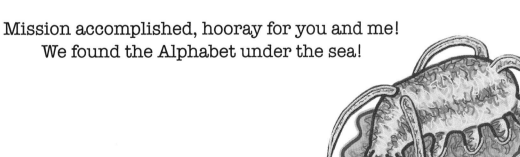

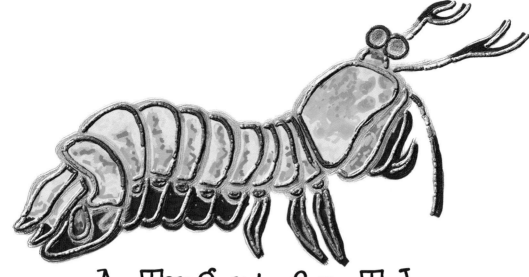

A Tangent for T.J.

T.J. the mantis shrimp
Is a colorful fellow
His shell of many colors
Blue, red and yellow
But that's just the start
Of his colorful facts
For inside of his head
The world's very abstract
He sees things brighter
Than we people do
Where we see green
He sees yellowish-blue
This fellow sees colors
Like a reddish type green
And purple much brighter
Than you've ever seen
They're impossible colors
The colors he views
Do you imagine he thinks
Of things like we do?
What if pink salmon
Are not really pink?
And the blue whale isn't
As blue as we think?
You can learn so much
From others who
See the world differently
Than the way you do

Prevail of the Snail

Home is where the heart is
Well, isn't that true
When you're a jeweled top snail
With your home stuck to you?
This shell has been with her
Since the day she hatched
Growing upon her
A high-rise on her back
She spends her days climbing
The kelp forest, so slow
It takes her a while
To get where she goes
But no matter the things
That weigh down her back
Or the things in the way
Slowing her path
She'll always keep snailing
And trailing on through
This snail never quits
And neither should you!

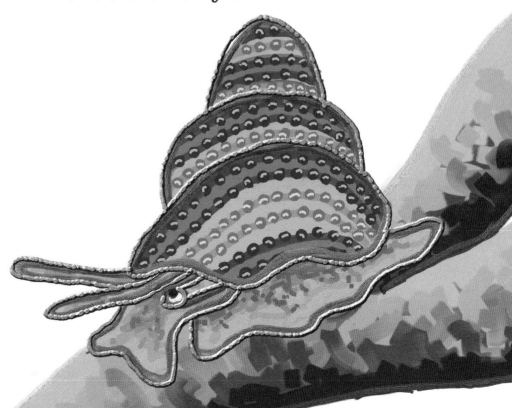

Whale Sharks Question Marks

We're here to solve the mystery
Of this gentle mammoth of the sea
Is she a whale or is she a shark?
Well, the answer to that question mark
Is she's much more sharky than a whale
From her giant mouth to her spotted tail
There is no blowhole upon her head
She breathes with her ten gills instead
She feeds on plankton, algae and krill
But I think I have more questions still
If she's a shark does that make her scary?
And not to mention the tooth fairy...
Has anyone told her about this mouth?
I think it's time she changes her route
This shark has three hundred rows of teeth
She never uses when she eats
And here is one last question mark
Is there such thing as a tooth fairy shark?

Undersea Library

Shhhh! You've reached the library
Our book filled place under the sea
Where magic happens under every cover
So, whether we have scales or blubber
An adventure waits on every page
Our imagination is the stage
Books aren't only words, you see
They take us fish where we can't be
Perhaps they will take squids to shore,
Whales to space, eels to explore
These books take us where we can't go
(Fish can't breath on shore, you know)
So, while you're down here in the sea
We're up in space or in a tree,
Driving cars, wearing pants
Or having picnics with the ants
Maybe we're reading all about you
While you are reading about us too!
For the world's much bigger than it looks
All you need is open books

Sensible Sea Urchin

If you wonder where
An urchin keeps her smile
You could look and look
And wonder for a while
Maybe you won't find it
For her smile's not on top
She keeps it underneath her
Burrowed in the rocks
And if you ask her why
She's living upside down
She'll say, "Now, wait a minute
You've got this turned around!

How are you so sure
I'm not turned the right way?
What if you're the one
Living life in disarray?
When it comes to the surface
And even the ground
How are you certain
That up is not down?
If I have these spines
And you don't have any
Do you have too little
Or do I have too many?
I have no eyes,
No scales and no fins
But if you have them all
Who really wins?
If we are both happy
With the way that we are
No matter what way
Seems most bizarre
Is there really an answer
That's worth a fight
How are you sure
That your way is right?
Everything depends
On your point of view
The way I see something
May be different than you
So, before you ask why
I have it all wrong
Ask yourself if you're sure
You were right all along"
Before questioning
Someone else's thoughts
Instead of asking why
Ask yourself why not?
For our world is most shaped
By those who are "strange"
But those who think different
Bring about the most change

I'm a Seal, You See

I am Sylvia the seal
I'm no sea lion at all
People tend to confuse us
The names we are called
True, we fin footed mammals
Are all named pinnipeds
But you can see the difference
Just by looking at our heads
Sea lions have earflaps
And us seals, just little holes
We are very different
Us swimming ocean souls
I have shorter flippers
Webbed with claws and hair
While those enormous sea lions
Have a naked flipper pair
They lay around and sunbath
Or walk along the shore
But I like staying in the sea
And swimming so much more
So you see, we're very different
Even though we seem the same
For a seal is not a seal
By any other name

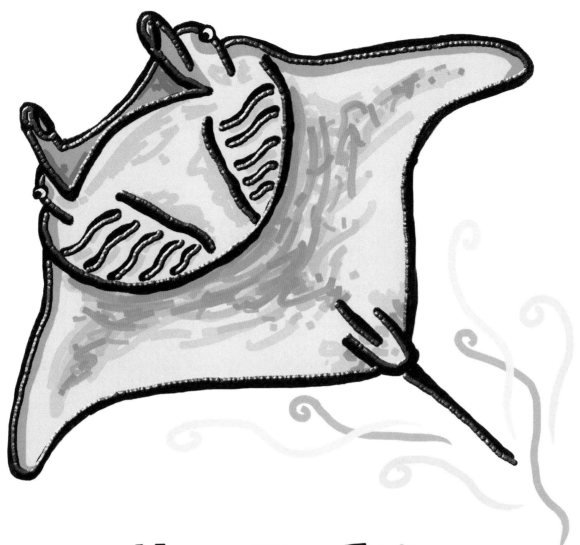

Manta Kite Flight

Like a kite blowing in a briny breeze
Soaring through the sapphire seas
Diving and dipping up and down
Touching tops and surfing grounds
Swooping, speeding, she never stills
Whooshing water through her gills
The manta ray is a splendid sight
A giant fish shaped like a kite
With fins stretching twenty feet wide
That propel her up, out of the tide
How can two fins take her that high?
Taking a leap's the only way to try!
Mantas don't wait for wind to soar
Just the courage to jump up from the floor
For you don't need wings to learn to fly
The only impossible things are the ones you don't try

Sea Slug Spiel

Has anyone told you
You are what you eat?
Well, I have some creatures
I'd like you to meet
Sea slugs that blend
With sponges and corals
All over the world
Among ocean florals
Absorbing their food
To store it inside
Taking on traits
Their habitat provides
Taking in colors
From things they eat
In order to hide
And blend with the treat
Some eat plants
Then act like their meal
Making food from the sun
Using traits they steal
Several store poison
From sponges they munch
In their tail as defense
So they don't become lunch
For they have just one foot
To use when they flee
So, they find unique ways
To survive in the sea
There are many facts
About sea slugs galore
So many, in fact
I think you need more
Slugs don't have noses
As well as no ears
Just horns on their heads
To smell and hear

They don't have bones
To support their shapes
Their bodies are blobby
And squishy like grapes
Sea slugs have no gills
Like fish in their scales
They don't breath like us
Not even like whales
Just a feathery crown
Fixed next to their tails
Help slugs breathe in
And even exhale
Sea slugs are neat
But catch a bad wrap
It's tough being a snail
With no shell on your back
Sure, slugs may be slimy
And squishy a tad
But being what you eat
Doesn't seem all that bad

Bully Blues

We like to think that sharks are the meanies of the sea
But what about the lionfish? Now, there's a real bully
With bright red stripes and sharp venomous spines
Flowing with his fins like a wicked warning sign
If he likes your reef, he'll come eat up all your food
Then scare off all your friends with his bad bully mood
And if nobody stands up to him how will he ever know
How he hurts other fishes in the sea down below?
Not saying anything is the worst thing you can do
Never stay silent when someone's mean to you
There is never an excuse for hurting someone else
But always a reason to stand up for yourself
If you see someone get bullied who is not you
Stand up, give your voice and speak for them too
All it ever takes is one person to protect them
Bullies only hurt you or others if you let them

Mystic Manatees

It is a silly story
How mermaids were thought up
By sailors in big boats
When there weren't planes and such
They looked into the water
And saw ladies in the sea
But what they thought were mermaids
Were really Manatees!
These pudgy little sea cows
Were the start of such a tale
At least that's how they tell it
Outside the realm of whales
But deep down in the sea
There's so much we don't know
Who says what is and isn't
In the places we can't gov

Snazzy Sea Otter

Stewart the furry otter
The water weasel of the sea
Is slipping on his coat
Dressing done up and fancy
He's going to the Otter Ball
To dance the weasel wiggle,
To trot the otter trotter
And jive a joyful jiggle
Until working up an appetite
He'll dive down for a rock
As otter party urchins
Only open with a knock
Then, when he's done and tired
He'll roll onto his back
To cuddle in the sea kelp
For a little otter nap

No Worries Whale

There is a tale of a happy whale
That never worried much
But I don't listen well as people tell
Tales and stories and such
Yes, there is a blurb that I have heard
About a worriless giant
But whether it's true or hullabaloo
I surely couldn't recite it
No, I don't know how the story goes
I won't even pretend
But it had a start, a middle part
And quite a splashy end

If that is not the story's plot
I wish that it were true
Because no whale in any tale
Should worry or be blue
But what I know of whales below
Is the mess we've left them to
The way, my friend, their story ends
Is really up to you!

A Statement From the Creators:

It is important to note that No Worries Whale is much more than a book. It is a tool. A tool that parents can use at home and teachers can use in their classrooms. These poems bring animals children don't always get to see right into their rooms and classrooms, providing the perfect way to make science and literacy accessible through poetry and art. We use fun facts about different ocean-dwellers and portray them in a sometimes serious and sometimes nonsensical style that will entertain children while educating them on the different species with which we share our planet. And as if that isn't enough, we also introduce children to important life lessons and conservation concepts such as recycling.

With that said, a question we are often asked is why we created this book? Why the ocean? And the answer is simple. Every child on this planet and every child of the future depends on clean air and clean water to survive. Every other breath we take comes from the ocean, so if we want to leave the world a better place for future generations, the best place to start is with the next one. We are passionate about education, we care about the generations that will come after we are gone and we value the lives that occupy our oceans. The sooner these creatures occupy the hearts of children, the sooner we foster a love for the ocean that encompasses up to eighty percent of all life on our planet. For, although we represent their greatest threat, we are also their greatest hope. We believe that the more children and their families know about our oceans, and the more they connect with the amazing creatures that inhabit them, the harder they will work to conserve them. Children need to know more than the how and why of recycling, they need to know who they are protecting by doing so. Every child has the power to change the world. All we need to do is give them the tools.

So in short, we created this book because we don't want there to be a last generation to see a whale, a last generation to swim in the ocean or a last generation with the chance to do something about it.

You will make a difference, or maybe you won't.
But who will do it if you don't?

Acknowledgements:

We want to thank all of the wonderful people who helped make the printing of No Worries Whale possible.

It will take all of us, and more, to teach and inspire children to love and protect our planet.

A special thanks to:

Benjamin • The Beukenhorst Family
The Brennan Family • Rich Brouillard • The Bryar Family
Your California Cousin • Kaitlynn Clifford
Cooper • The Douglass/Kesting Family
Henry James Flores • Violet Lucille Flores
Becky and Bill Gehrke • Megan Gehrke
The Grove Family • Ashley Nichole Hasna
Grayson Herr • The Hinnerichs Family
The Hohn Family • Molly Hohn • Noah Hohn
Brendan Holden • Connor Holden • Kayley Holden
Arielle and Jason • Shannon Jenkins
Amy Jo Johnson • The Jorgensen Family • Ingrid Kunz
Ashlyn Landis • Patty Landis • Samantha Landis
Jan Limbo • Phil Manley • Kathy McGinty
Mertzgomery • The Montgomery Family
Janice and Gene Montgomery
Andrew Mortensen and Julian • Marcy Mortensen
In Memory of Larry Woodrow Mortensen
Kim Nelson • Jameson Wesley Neve • Barbara Nock
Henry James Paulson • Jack Michael Paulson • Penelope Rae
The Melvin Ronning family in memory of Doris and Mabel Ronning
Lexy Ronning • Lisa Ronning • Valerie Ronning
Zephaniah Savage • Addy Schmidt • sciencewithhiggins.com
Scuba Squirrel • Josie Shannon • Liam Shannon
Brad Sojka • Brian Sojka • Cheryl Sojka • David Sojka • Jim Sojka
Don, Ely and Elseanne Staniford • The Richard Stensaas Family •
Valley Boys Roofing • Wendy Walsh

Other Works:

Amanda Gehrke and Allison Sojka's next project is a similar book:

No Frets Froggy: a book of rainforest poems

Because whales shouldn't have to worry, and frogs shouldn't have to fret either.

Made in the USA
Charleston, SC
04 November 2013